P9-DVB-599

HILLSBORO PUBLIC LIBRARIES
Hillsboro, OR
Member of Washington County
COOPERATIVE LIBRARY SERVICES

WITHDRAWN

A Note to Parents

DK READERS is a compelling program for beginning readers, designed in conjunction with leading literacy experts, including Dr. Linda Gambrell, Professor of Education at Clemson University. Dr. Gambrell has served as President of the National Reading Conference, the College Reading Association, and the International Reading Association.

Beautiful illustrations and superb full-color photographs combine with engaging, easy-to-read stories to offer a fresh approach to each subject in the series. Each DK READER is guaranteed to capture a child's interest while developing his or her reading skills, general knowledge, and love of reading.

The five levels of DK READERS are aimed at different reading abilities, enabling you to choose the books that are exactly right for your child:

Pre-level 1: Learning to read
Level 1: Beginning to read
Level 2: Beginning to read alone
Level 3: Reading alone
Level 4: Proficient readers

The "normal" age at which a child begins to read can be anywhere from three to eight years old. Adult participation through the lower levels is very helpful for providing encouragement, discussing storylines, and sounding out unfamiliar words.

No matter which level you select, you can be sure that you are helping your child learn to read, then read to learn!

LONDON, NEW YORK, MUNICH,
MELBOURNE, AND DELHI

For DK Publishing
Designer Owen Bennett
Managing Art Editor Ron Stobbart
Managing Editor Catherine Saunders
Art Director Lisa Lanzarini
Publishing Manager Simon Beecroft
Category Publisher Alex Allan
Production Editor Sean Daly
Production Controller Rita Sinha
Reading Consultant Dr. Linda Gambrell

For Lucasfilm
Executive Editor J. W. Rinzler
Editor Frank Parisi
Art Director Troy Alders
Keeper of the Indycron Leland Chee
Director of Publishing Carol Roeder

First published in the United States in 2011
by DK Publishing
375 Hudson Street, New York, New York 10014

11 12 13 14 15 10 9 8 7 6 5 4 3 2 1

Copyright © 2011 Lucasfilm Ltd and ™
All rights reserved. Used under authorization.

Page design copyright © 2011 Dorling Kinderley Limited

176028—10/10

All rights reserved under International and Pan-American Copyright Conventions. No part of this publication may be reproduced, stored in a retrieval system, or transmitted in any form or by any means, electronic, mechanical, photocopying, recording, or otherwise, without the prior written permission of the copyright owner.
Published in Great Britain by Dorling Kindersley Limited

DK books are available at special discounts when purchased in bulk for sales promotions, premiums, fund-raising, or educational use.
For details, contact:
DK Publishing Special Markets
375 Hudson Street
New York, New York 10014
SpecialSales@dk.com

A catalog record for this book is available
from the Library of Congress.
4804 0303 4/12
ISBN 978-0-7566-7138-9 (Paperback)
ISBN 978-0-7566-7137-2 (Hardcover)

Color reproduction by Media Development and Printing Ltd, UK
Printed and bound in China by L.Rex

Discover more at

www.dk.com

www.indianajones.com

Contents

4 Treasure hunter
6 Young explorer
8 Along for the ride
10 Transport tales
12 Read all about it
14 Far and wide
18 Unlocking secrets
20 Finding clues
22 Treasure rivals
24 Watch out!
26 Strong personality
28 Helping hand
32 Treasure dangers!
38 Hidden treasure
42 Precious treasure
44 Beyond treasure
46 Secret treasure
48 Glossary

DK READERS

PROFICIENT 4 READERS

INDIANA JONES

HILLSBORO PUBLIC LIBRARIES
Hillsboro, OR
Member of Washington County
COOPERATIVE LIBRARY SERVICES

THE SEARCH FOR BURIED TREASURE

Written by W. Rathbone

Treasure hunter

The search for buried treasure is ifficult and it can be dangerous. ortunately, Indiana Jones has some ecial skills. Over the years he has und many legendary treasures ncluding the Ark of the Covenant, e sacred Sankara Stones, the Holy rail, and an alien Crystal Skull.

Indy loves searching for rare rtifacts. He also enjoys solving ysteries and traveling around e world. Indy has cut through eserts, jungles, and rain forests. e has also explored castles, mples, and secret tombs. owever, he has learned at sometimes the most vilized places can be e most dangerous.

Dr. Jones
Indy's real name is Dr. Henry Jones, Jr. When he is not busy searching for treasure, he works as a professor of archaeology.

an elegant Shanghai ghtclub, Indy wears a stylish hite suit, but has to evade ath several times!

Dr. Henry Jones
Indy inherited his name and also his love of history from his father, a professor of medieval literature.

Young explorer

Indy has always loved to explore, even from a young age. During a visit to Egypt, young Indy found his way into an old tomb. It was the tomb of Ka, an ancient king. In the tomb, Indy found his first buried treasure: the sculpted head of a jackal.

Now Indy is much older, but his ove of searching for rare artifacts as strong as ever. He continues is search for treasures whenever e can. Sometimes his son, Mutt, elps him out. Together Indy and Iutt traveled to Peru to look hrough an underground crypt for he mummy of a Spanish explorer.

Marion Ravenwood
Marion and Indy have known each other for many years. They had several adventures together before getting married.

Henry "Mutt" Jones III
Indy and Marion have a son, known as "Mutt." Mutt prefers working on his motorcycle to studying, but he is impressed by his father's adventures.

Humpy ride
On a trip to the deserts of Egypt, young Indy learned how to ride a camel.

Along for the ride

The quest for exotic treasures often takes Indy to remote places where there are no proper roads or any modern forms of transportation. Indy has had to learn how to get around on all kinds of animals.

Indy and his friends were given elephants to ride when on the trail of the Sankara Stones in India. The elephants had a peculiar odor. Indy was not bothered by the smell, but his friend Willie did not like it. She doused her elephant with perfume to make it smell nicer!

On horseback
As a Boy Scout, Indy enjoyed a lot of horseback riding and got a taste of adventure.

Willie Scott
Wilhelmina "Willie" Scott is a nightclub singer who first met Indiana Jones in Shanghai.

On the road in India, Indy rides an elephant in search of the Sankara Stones.

Indy tells Short Round and Willie to hold on for dear life!

Family trip
In Peru, Marion drove while Mutt watched his dad eliminate traffic in front of them—with a bazooka!

Transport tales

Indiana Jones often travels great distances. Over the years he has ha to drive, pilot, or just hang on to a variety of vehicles. Sometimes Indy needs to get somewhere in a hurry, but other times he needs to make a fast getaway using whatever vehicle he can find. To escape the Temple of Doom, he jumped into a mine car with his friends Willie and Short Round.

During another
etaway Indy stole
motorcycle—and
is dad rode in the
decar. Nazis were
hasing them so Indy
anted to get far away.
lowever, Indy's father
anted them to go to the Nazi
eadquarters in Berlin!
lenry knew that he would find his
iary there and that it would lead
nem to the priceless Holy Grail.

Air adventure
The Jones' journey from Berlin involved a biplane, with Indy's dad in charge of the machine gun.

dy and his father do not always
ree on everything.

Father always knows best
Indy might have been steering the motorcycle, but Henry told his son which way to go—straight to their enemies' headquarters.

Vacation reading
Young Indy took books to read while on a trip in Kenya, Africa.

Read all about it

Indiana Jones has always loved to read, especially history books. He knows many things about ancient cultures and civilizations. This knowledge is very useful when he is hunting for rare artifacts.

Young Indy reads with his friend Meto of the Kenyan Massai tribe.

dy enjoys teaching others about history.

Indy has also mastered many
nguages, including Latin and
anskrit, to help him in his search
or elusive treasures.
His knowledge of
ncient texts helped
im to find the
acred Ark of the
Covenant before
nyone else.

Ark of the Covenant
The Ark is where the prophet Moses is believed to have placed the list of ancient biblical rules known as the Ten Commandments.

Ark book
This illustration shows the power of the Ark. It could destroy whole armies!

Patient teacher
During his early travels, Indy was taught by his patient and wise tutor, Helen.

Young explorer
In India, Indy encountered a young philosopher named Krishnamurti.

Far and wide

The search for buried treasure take Indiana Jones all over the globe. He tours many countries and cities, visiting temples, churches, and monuments. One adventure in India lead Indy to a hidden temple where he had to do battle with an evil pries to uncover the Sankara Stones.

Indy took his son, Mutt, on his first
reat adventure—to South America
search of an alien artifact.
a marketplace in Peru, Mutt
nd Indy began their search for an
ncient explorer, and the hidden
rystal Skull. As usual, Indy wasn't
e only one looking for this
owerful treasure.

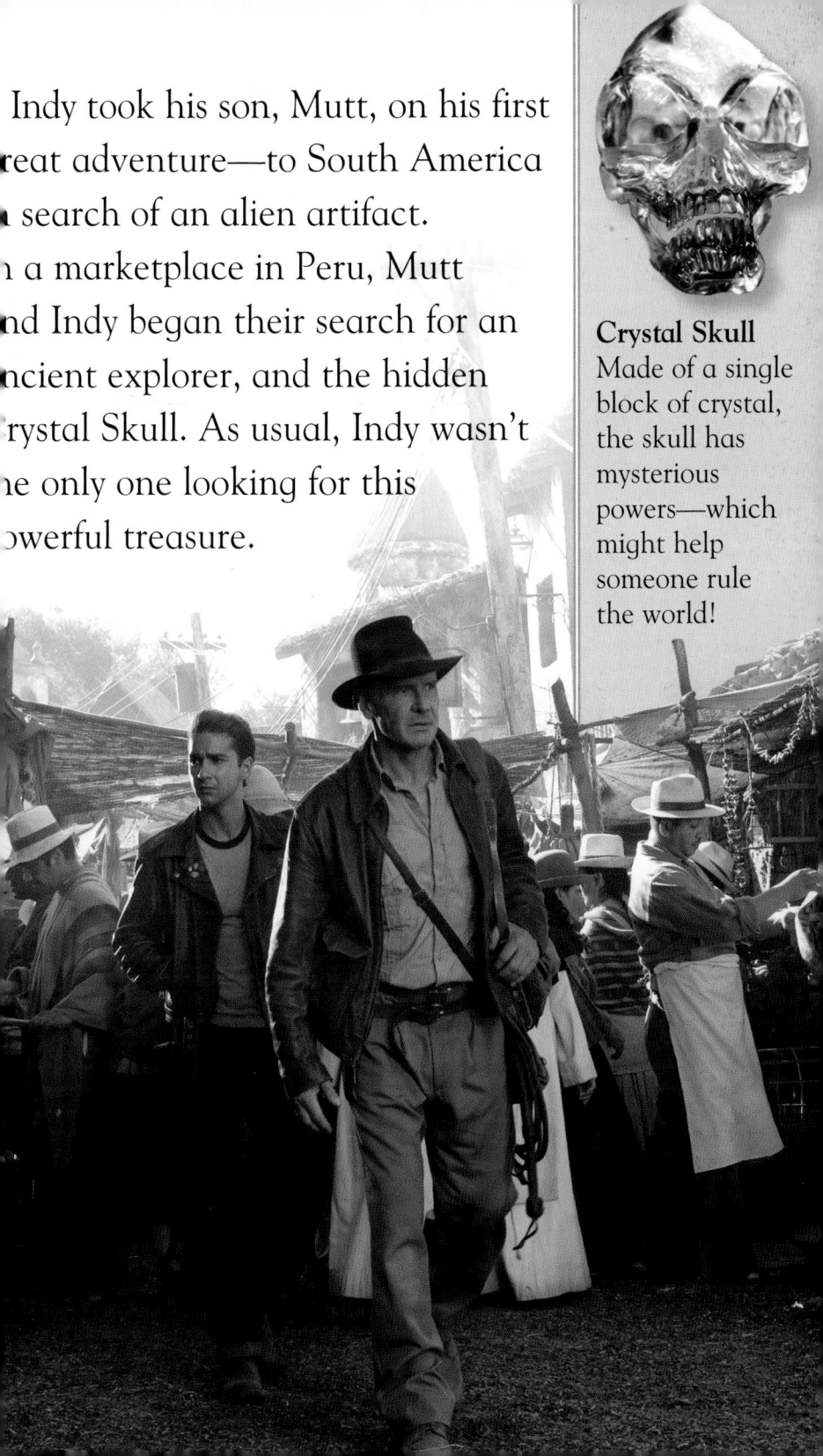

Crystal Skull
Made of a single block of crystal, the skull has mysterious powers—which might help someone rule the world!

Abner Ravenwood
Marion Ravenwood's father, Abner, devoted his life to studying texts and objects relating to the Ark of the Covenant.

When Indy was hunting for the Ark of the Covenant, his quest took him to a desolate snowy mountain in Nepal, Asia. He was determined to find the sacred treasure before the Nazis and hoped that his old teacher Abner Ravenwood could help him. The Nazis thought that the power of the Ark would destroy their enemies, but Indy wasn't about to let that happen!

Indy hoped to find a clue that vould lead him to the Ark—the eadpiece of Ra. In a tiny village avern he found his old friend Marion Ravenwood. Indy learned hat Marion's father was dead. Unfortunately some Nazi thugs also rrived, determined to fight Indy for he headpiece. During their struggle, fire was started and the tavern urned down. The Nazis fled but ndy escaped with the headpiece.

ndy must use his rain as well as his rength to outsmart ne Nazi thugs.

Nazis
Arnold Toht was a Nazi agent.
The Nazis were the ruling party of Germany between 1933 and 1945.

Close call
Indy is nearly choked, shot, and set on fire. However, thanks to his quick thinking—and a little help from Marion—Indy survives.

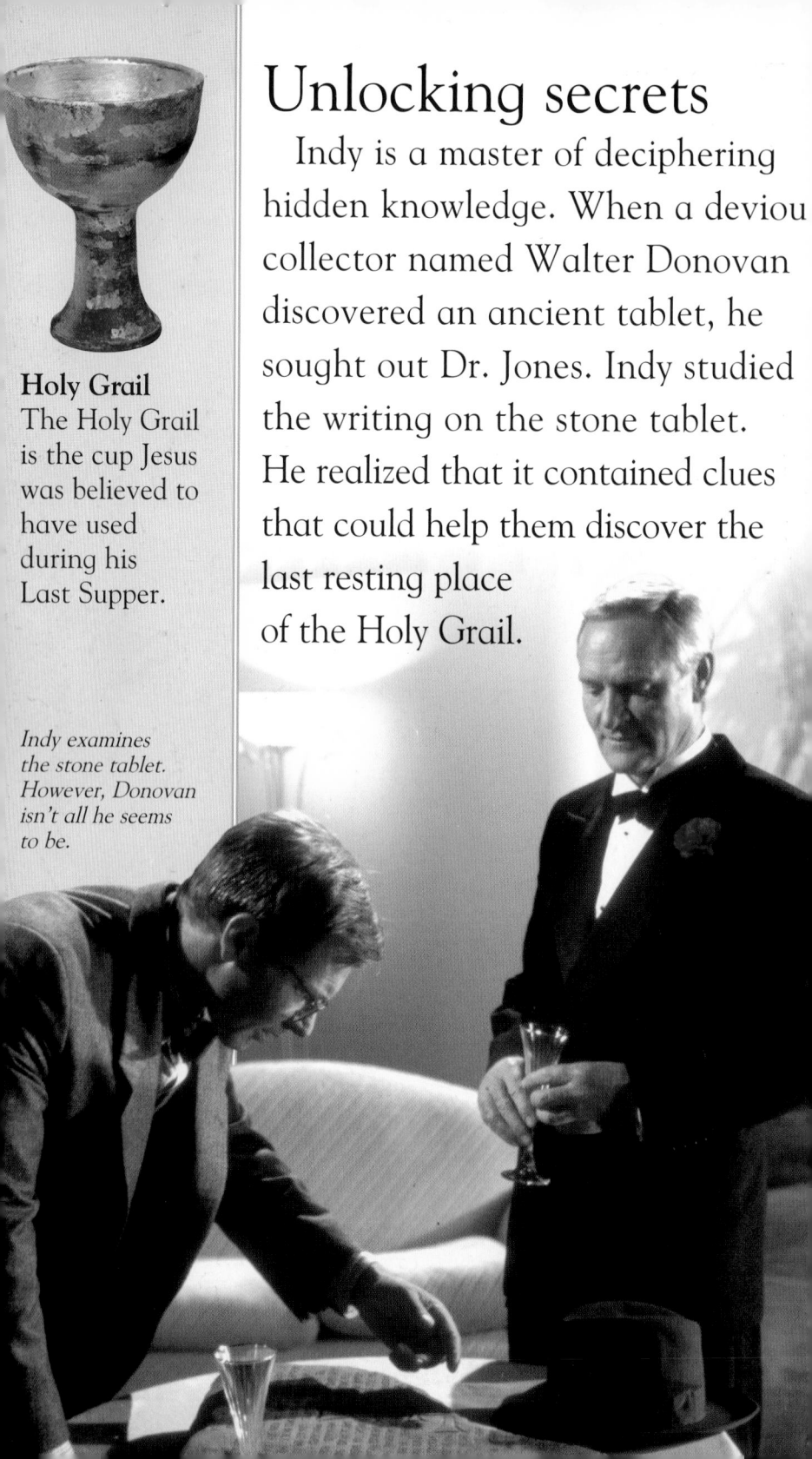

Holy Grail
The Holy Grail is the cup Jesus was believed to have used during his Last Supper.

Unlocking secrets

Indy is a master of deciphering hidden knowledge. When a deviou collector named Walter Donovan discovered an ancient tablet, he sought out Dr. Jones. Indy studied the writing on the stone tablet. He realized that it contained clues that could help them discover the last resting place of the Holy Grail.

Indy examines the stone tablet. However, Donovan isn't all he seems to be.

However, sometimes even
)r. Jones needs help to
nderstand ancient clues.
)uring his quest to find the Ark,
ıdy needed help from an expert
strologer to decode the ancient
ıarkings of the headpiece of Ra.
'he wise man was able to tell
ıdy the correct height for the
taff on which he should place the
eadpiece to help him find the Ark.

Headpiece of Ra
The fabulous headpiece is adorned with mysterious symbols and writings on both sides. Only an expert can decipher its clues.

Finding clues

Whether sneaking through perilous jungles or carefully searching dusty libraries, Indy has to decipher many different clues and signs Sometimes important clues will be incomplete or damaged.

When Indy was looking for treasure hidden in an ancient temple, he found half of an old map. He bargained with a colleague to get the second half and then used his skil to find the treasure.

Maps
Many maps are incredibly detailed, but Indy often has to rely on extremely simple or ancient maps made by amateurs: Is that a path or a dangerous cliff?

Sometimes clues are carefully idden, but other times they might e staring Indy in the face. In an d library in Italy, Indy was looking r the entrance to an even older ypt. Here, "X" marked the spot. ndy found the secret world beneath ne library, although he had to reak through the floor without lerting the librarian! Far below, mong the crumbling skeletons, ndy hoped to find another clue ading to the Holy Grail.

Crypt
Crypts are hidden chambers, usually underground. Indy found a marker in a crypt pointing toward the Holy Grail.

Longtime enemy
René Belloq is a rival archaeologist who cares only for money and power.

Arab dress
Most Arab countries are hot, so people must wear loose clothes to keep them cool. Indy's flowing robes and headdress also made a great disguise!

Treasure rivals

The search for treasure can often lead Indy straight into danger. That is because his enemies are searching for the same thing—and they will stop at nothing to get it. It is often a race against time between Indy and the bad guys. Because he is resourceful and never gives up, Indy usually wins.

During the hunt for the Ark of the Covenant, Indy disguised himself as an Arab tribesman to avoid being caught by Nazis. Then he used a rope to descend into a concealed Map Room without anyone noticing him.

In the Map Room, Indy placed the headpiece of Ra on a precisely measured staff. Clever Indy was now one step ahead of the Nazis!

Hieroglyphics
The walls of the Map Room are covered in an ancient Egyptian language that used pictures known as hieroglyphics to convey words.

Found it!
When sunlight shone through the headpiece, it magically illuminated the chamber where the Ark of the Covenant lay hidden.

No fear
Young Indy had no fear of snakes. When his friend was frightened by a snake, Indy grabbed the critter and tossed it aside.

Watch out!

Precious artifacts are often guarded. Sometimes they are protected by deadly traps and snares, other times they are patroled by fearsome animals. Indy is not frightened of nasty snares or dangerous booby traps, but there is one thing he is terrified of—snakes.

New fear
Indy developed a phobia after falling into a crate of snakes. Since then he has really hated them.

On his quest for the ankara Stones in the Temple f Doom Indy came face to ce with a snake. Was it real a statue? Indy looked away nd when he turned back, e mysterious snake had anished into thin air!

Rats!
Indy's father does not have a problem with snakes, but he does hate rats. When Indy encountered hundreds of rats in a crypt, he remarked that his dad would have been scared to death!

Sankara Stones
Legend says there are five sacred stones. When they are close to each other, the diamonds within glow mysteriously.

Chilled monkey brains
Willie had been really looking forward to dinner.
She declined the bugs and when offered brains instead, she fainted.

Strong personality

Sometimes Indy needs a strong arm and an even stronger stomach to seek out precious treasure.

The search for the buried Sankara Stones led Indiana and his friends Willie and Short Round to Pankot Palace. It seemed like a very civilized place. Indy met royalty, ministers, officers, rich guests—and ate very scary food. When Indy and Willie attended a great banquet they were served boiled black beetles, eyeball soup, and python, poached and stuffed with live baby eels!

After dinner, things got worse for ndy. He returned to his room and vas attacked, and he soon liscovered that children were eing used to dig for the Sankara Stones. Indy was letermined to save hem, but first he had to face the uardians of a inister temple—he Thuggees!

Thuggees
The Temple of Doom was controlled by a group known as Thuggees who worshipped the goddess Kali.

Helping hand

Even Indiana Jones sometimes need a helping hand. In fact, Indy needs al the friends he can get during his man perilous adventures! Some of Indy's friends are loyal, but some of them are not so loyal.

In the jungles of India, Indy and his friend Short Round cheated eacl other at cards. But when it counted, Short Round saved Dr. Jones's life.

Best friend
During his adventures as a young man, Indy often needed help from his good friend Rémy.

Short Round
Indy found the orphan Short Round in Shanghai. He turned out to be a very good pal, and helped Indy escape from a gambling club.

Walter Donovan, however, only
retended to be Indy's friend.
Ie wanted the Holy Grail at any
ost and used Indy's skills to find it.
'hen Donovan turned his guns on
ne adventurer and claimed his prize.

Walter Donovan
Donovan posed as Indy's friend, but he was willing to injure Indy's father to get what he wanted.

Deadly friend
Donovan was betrayed himself by someone he thought was his friend. Elsa Schneider tricked him into drinking from the wrong cup, killing him!

Sallah
Sallah has gone on many adventures with Indy. He lives in Cairo and helped his friend dig up the Ark of the Covenant.

Although his friends have often saved his life, Indy has also come to the rescue of his pals many times. He was not sure if Elsa Schneider was his friend or enemy, but when she was threatened by a Nazi he preferred not to take any chances.

Indy is beginning to wish that he hadn't trusted Elsa Schneide

Elsa
Dr. Elsa Schneider is a double agent. She is willing to help Indy as long as his work benefits her—and her Nazi employers.

His father told Indy that Elsa was Nazi, but Indy was torn. He threw own his gun so that Elsa would not e harmed but in the next instant he alized his mistake. She was a Nazi! dy learned the hard way that he ould have listened to his father.

Marcus Brody
Marcus is a friend to both Indy and his father. He runs a museum and sends Indy on many missions to retrieve ancient objects.

George "Mac" McHale
Mac is also a double agent. When he is in debt, he will work for anyone, even if it means harming his friend Indy.

Golden idol
The ancient Chachapoyans created a golden fertility idol. Many explorers had met their death trying to acquire it.

Treasure dangers!

The best part of searching for hidden treasures is the thrill of discovery. This exciting moment, however, often is extremely dangerous—treasure does not always want to be found!

When Indy finally located a golden idol in an ancient temple, h slowly reached out to collect his priz

The idol sits on a pressure-sensitive disk—if the idol is taken, deadly traps are sprung!

However, by lifting the idol, Indy set ff many traps. First he had to avoid oison darts, then he had to leap over bottomless chasm. Next his friend etrayed him and then an enormous oulder came crashing toward him! inally, Indy threw himself eadlong through spider webs nto the jungle outside. Jnfortunately, Belloq was aiting there to take the idol. etter luck next time, Indy!

Treasure thief Belloq used members of the Hovito tribe to help him retrieve the idol from Indy.

Indy uses surveying tools like transits and levels to pinpoint the Ark's location.

More snakes
Indy was less than pleased to see the floor appear to be writhing—it was covered in thousands of pythons and cobras!

The search for the Ark was also extremely dangerous. It took Indy to North Africa, where he located the area under which the valuable artifact lay. His enemies slept all around him, but Indy told his men to start digging in the desert sand. The sky turned dark and lightning split the clouds. It seemed as if nature itself was angry!

After digging through the night, Indy descended through an opening to find the powerful buried treasure.

Buried alive
Cruel Gestapo agent Toht pushed Marion into the antique tomb and sealed her in with Indy. He hoped they enjoyed their living death!

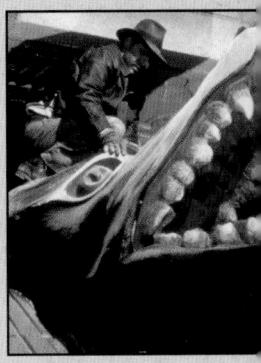

Jackal god
Indy had to climb an enormous statue of a jackal to escape and pursue the Ark, which was taken by the Nazis.

True test
Indy had to avoid deadly traps on his way to the Grail room. At one point, huge circular blades threatened to cut him in two!

Faith
Indy had to summon all of his faith to take a step into what looked like a bottomless chasm.

On another occasion, Indy discovered the last resting place of the Holy Grail, but found more than one cup. He had to use all of his learning and instincts to work out which cup was the true Grail.

Choosing the wrong cup
ould result in a horrible death.
ortunately, Indy remembered
hat Jesus was a modest man
o he would not have used a
ewel-encrusted vessel.

Wrong cup
Donovan followed Indy to the Grail room and chose poorly. The result? Instant aging into dust!

Right cup
Before his father drank from the Grail, Indy had to make sure it was the right cup. Phew! Indy's instincts were correct.

Grail knight
The bravest Crusader was one of three brothers who had sworn to protect the Holy Grail.

Hidden treasure

The word "treasure" can mean many things. It can be a valuable idol or a precious relic, but it can also mean something, or someone, much closer to home. Finding the Grail cup meant that once again Indy had triumphed over his enemie and it also made him realize how much he loved his father.

When the wicked Donovan shot Henry, Indy had to enter the Grail sanctuary to save his father.

The Grail knight greets Indy after guarding the Grail for 700 years.

After finding the true Grail cup, ndy poured water from it into his ather's wound. Miraculously it ealed almost instantly. Henry felt s good as new, which was a good hing because Elsa was about to nake a dangerous mistake!

Naughty Elsa
Elsa couldn't resist the promise of immortality so she grabbed the Grail and ran for the exit.

Grail diary
Thanks to his father's detailed diary, Indy was able to locate the Holy Grail.

Wise father Henry Sr. knew that the cave would collapse if anyone walked over the floor's Great Seal with the Grail.

Some treasures are just not meant to be kept. When Elsa Schneider tried to take the Holy Grail out of the cave, she triggered an earthquake. Indy tried to save her, but Elsa's desire for the Grail was too great and she fell into a chasm.

The Grail lay perched on a ledge
lmost within reach, so Indy tried
grab it. He stretched with all his
ight but the earthquake was
educing the cave to rubble.
ndy wisely chose to save his own
fe, rather than recapture the Grail.

Compassion
Indy was willing to forgive Elsa for trying to kill him but Elsa was determined to get the Grail so she let go of Indy's hand.

On the run
His strength returned, Henry was led out of the cave by Indy to their waiting horses. They then rode into the sunset.

Cross of Coronado
While on a Boy Scout outing, Indy discovered grave robbers just as they unearthed a fabled golden crucifix.

Precious treasure

Finding rare artifacts can be just th beginning of the story. What happen afterward can sometimes be almost a much of an adventure! Indiana Jones believes that most treasures should be kept safe, and that, in most cases, the best place for them is in a museum.

As a young man, Indy resolved to return the Cross of Coronado to a museum. It took him many years to d so, but he eventually succeeded.

After Indy found the three
ankara Stones, he knew
hat he had to do the right
hing. Although two were
ost in his final battle with
n evil priest, he returned one
f them to its village home.
Vithout the stone, the people
ere starving and ragged, but with
he return of the sacred stone—and
heir children—the people thrived
nce again.

Mola Ram
Thuggee high priest Mola Ram enslaved children so they could dig beneath the Temple of Doom for the Sankara Stones.

World War I
Between 1914 and 1918 the Allied powers, including France, Britain, the USA, and Russia, fought World War I against Germany.

Beyond treasure

The adventures of Indiana Jones could fill a whole library. However, Indy is more than just a great teacher and a brave treasure hunter. During World War I, young Indy joined the Belgian army to fight against Germany and its allies. The horrible warfare in the trenches was his most terrifying ordeal.

Indy also fought in
/orld War II. He was
soldier and an
ıtelligence agent,
orking against the Nazis
nd their allies. After that,
ıdy was involved in the Cold
/ar. When the Russians pursued the
rystal Skull, Indy leaped into action
find it first. After all, finding treasure
what Indiana Jones does best.

World War II
Between 1939 and 1945 World War II was fought between the Axis powers, which included Germany, Japan, and Italy, and the Allies, which included Britain, France, and the United States of America.

The Cold War
After World War II relations were tense between Communist countries in the East, such as the Soviet Union, and countries in the West, such as the USA.

Secret treasure

Some treasures are too dangerous to be displayed in a museum. Although Indy traveled around the world and risked his life several times to obtain the Ark of the Covenant, no one would ever know about it.

Souvenirs
Indy's classroom contains many mementos of his adventures, including a sacred mask and an ancient carving.

Area 51
Rumor has it that the Ark is stored in the infamous Area 51, a top secret US military base in Nevada.

Some mysterious yet powerful
eople decided that the Ark
ust be hidden. So it was
aled in a crate and stored
a gigantic warehouse.
s location remains a closely
uarded secret, known only
a few people.

Further adventures
In his trademark fedora, Indy has become a legend—but for him life is the greatest adventure!

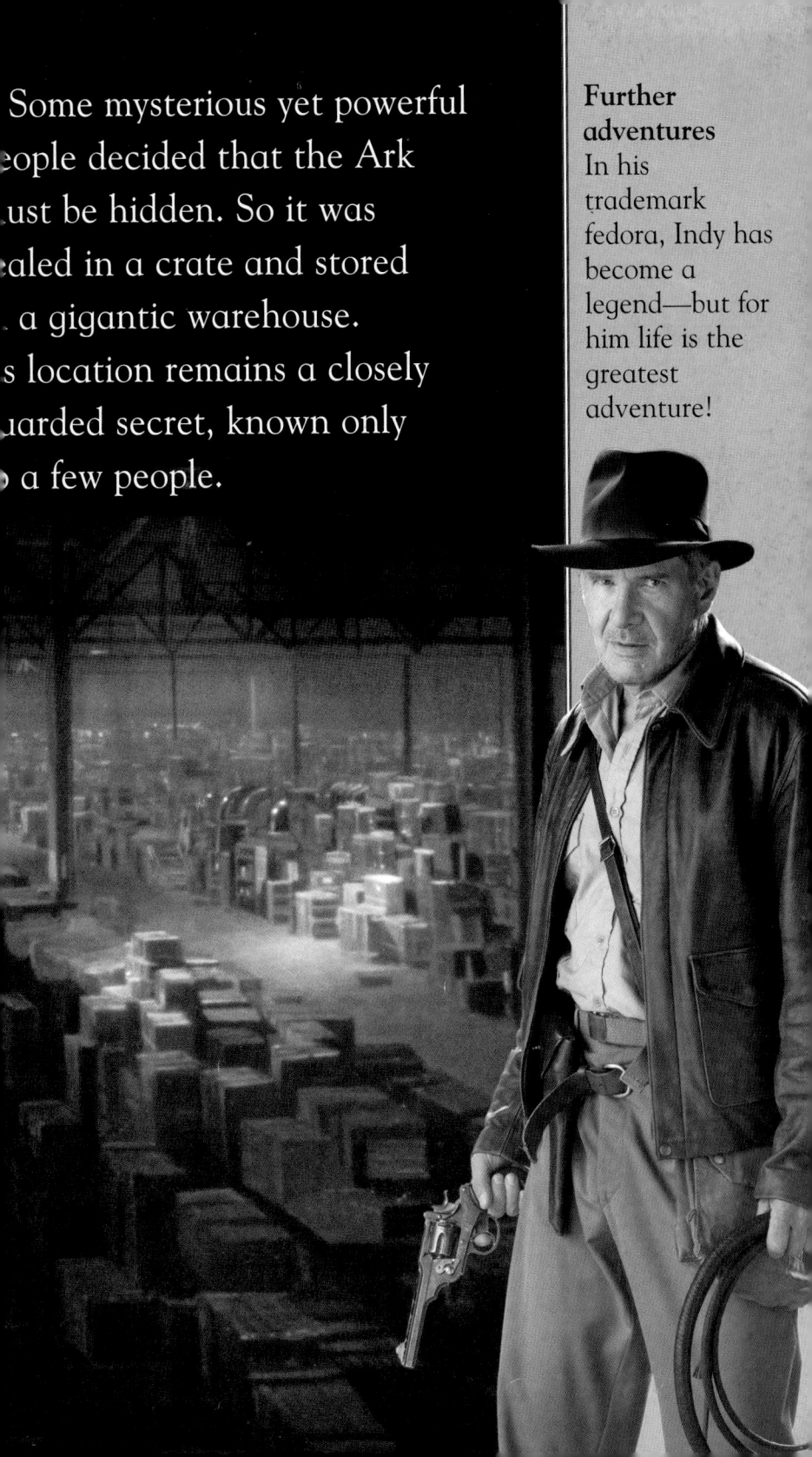

Glossary

Allies
People on the same side in a war.

Archaeology
The study of ancient life and objects.

Artifacts
Man-made objects, often from the past.

Bazooka
A handheld weapon that can fire rockets.

Booby trap
An explosive device that is set off when a harmless-looking object is touched.

Chasm
A deep crack in the ground.

Civilized
A society that has developed culturally.

Communist
A country whose government controls everything that is produced so that everyone has equal wealth.

Decipher
To work out the meaning of something.

Double agent
A spy who pretends to work for one government but works for another.

Elusive
Difficult to find.

Fedora
A soft felt hat.

Idol
A statue that is worshipped as a god.

Immortality
The ability to live forever.

Intelligence agent
A spy who collects information about an enemy.

Jackal
An animal that is similar to a dog.

Mementos
Objects kept to remember an event.

Mummy
A dead body that is wrapped in cloth before it is buried.

Perilous
With a risk of great danger.

Phobia
A great fear of something.

Relic
A precious part of something old that has remained.

Sacred
Something holy.

Sanctuary
A holy or safe place.

Sanskrit
An extinct language of ancient India.

Tomb
A cave used for burial.